I0632845

Georgine Tollet

Country Conversations

Georgine Tollet

Country Conversations

ISBN/EAN: 9783337227067

Printed in Europe, USA, Canada, Australia, Japan

Cover: Foto ©Andreas Hilbeck / pixelio.de

More available books at **www.hansebooks.com**

COUNTRY

CONVERSATIONS.

LONDON:

PRINTED BY

WHITING & CO., 30 & 32, SARDINIA STREET,

LINCOLN'S INN FIELDS.

1886.

CONTENTS.

PREFACE.

THESE Conversations were written down, as soon as possible after they were spoken, by one who, living for nearly fifty years in a country home, had cultivated habits of the most friendly intimacy with her neighbours. Whatever interest these records may have, arises from the fact that they are not the work of an inventive genius. The writer had a singularly accurate memory, a sense of quiet humour, and keen powers of observation; but of the faculty which creates she had no share. Her sole object was to preserve the exact expressions of those whose histories of themselves and of their affairs she had found so interesting. She scrupulously avoided making any additions or changes, though she sometimes omitted trifling de-tails, and recorded as little as possible of her own share in the dialogue.

These manuscripts were often a source of amusement to a circle of relations and intimate friends, and they are now preserved in a more convenient form for a younger generation.

March 1881.

COUNTRY CONVERSATIONS.

MRS. HARLAND.

1857.

Miss G. and Mrs. Harland, a farmer's wife, sitting in a comfortable farmhouse kitchen.

Mrs. H.—Mary, my daughter, said I must give her *love* to you, Miss G. You must please to excuse it, for she could not find any other word to shuit her.

Mary is a very good, prudent girl. She says to me, one day as she was breaking the curd, 'Mother, I will never let loose my affections on no man till I have proven him to be pious and in good circum-stances.'

I

For you know, Miss G., one will not do without the other; but indeed, men is so crafty one can't find out what their circumstances really is. Why, there's my daughter Anne's husband; I never could fancy him. He has too low a mind for me. And such a big unmannerly fellow! Why, Anne did not reach above his elbow; and a cast in his eye and all! But I thought his circumstances were good. He said he killed twice a week; and that looked well. So I persuaded my husband to give his consent to the marriage; but the very first time as I went to see them, Anne says to me, 'Mother, we're worsening in money every week; and if you can't help us, I shall soon be in the 'Sylum.'

Eh, dear! I thought I should have fainted; and I says to Anne, 'This comes of pushing past your father.' So I goes back to my husband, and tells him all that had passed ; but he set his face like a stone against me, and never spoke so much as one word. Well! I tried him again, night and day, twenty times ; but never a word could I get. So I says to myself, 'I'll just turn it over to the Lord'; and before I had prayed to Him a week that He would open a path for me, my husband was thrown out of a gig and broke his leg all to pieces, and I soon perceived that this would be the means of softening his heart.

So one day, when he was a bit better, I says to him, 'Hugh, you'll never be the man you have been, and you had better give up the malt-kin to Goodman ; for that's what the Lord means by this misfortune.' And he said 'Mary, you're right'; just so.

I felt that I had been very faithless,

Miss G., for being so troubled; for indeed when I got up in the morning, I was forced to cross my arms tight over my chest, to keep myself from falling to pieces. I will say this for Anne: she couldn't behave kinder to her husband if he had thousands a year coming in.

Miss G.—How are your sons going on?

Mrs. H.—My son Tom, Miss G., has met with a disappointment about getting married. You know he's got that nice farm at Hallwood; so he met a yong lady at a dance as he was very much took up with, and she seemed quite agreeable; so as he heard she had Five Hundred he wrote next day to purshue the acquaintance, and her father wrote and asked Tom to come over to Southwick. Eh, dear! poor fellow! he went off in such sperrits, and he looked so spruce in his best clothes, with a new tie and all. So next day, when I heard him come to the gate, I ran out as pleased as could be; but I see in a moment he was sadly cast down.

'Why, Tom, my lad,' says I, 'what is it?' 'Why, mother,' says he, 'she'd understood mine was a harable; and she *will* *not* marry to a dairy.'

———⚹———

1859.

Miss G. and Mrs. Harland in the same place.

Mrs. H.—My son George has been getting into a great scrape. You'll perhaps laugh when I tell you what it was, Miss G. But indeed he got himself engaged (as one may call it) to two sisters at onst.

It came about through a very remarkable

circum-stance. He'd been thinking of Jane
Thornton, the youngest sister, for some time.
So one day he says to me, 'Mother, the grey
horse has nothing to do to-day, and I'll
take him over to Hurst and speak to Jane
about getting married. I'll be back in
good time, because the horse must rest
before his journey to Oldcastle to-morrow.'

So he went; and he was back still sooner
than I expected. The moment I saw him
I thought something was amiss; and he
said, in rather a mournful voice, 'Mother,
I've got engaged to Caroline instead of
Jane.' 'Why, my lad,' says I, 'whatever
could you be so soft for?' 'Why,' says
he, 'when I got to Hurst, I found Jane
was gone to her aunt's, three or four miles
off, and I could not go after her, for the
horse was tired, and he must go a journey
for malt in the morning; so Caroline and

me, we've settled it, and you must ask them both to come here on a visit.'

Well, Miss G., there seemed no help for it. So I wrote; and they was here a week. So when the door was fairly shut on them I said, 'Now, George, can't you see that nothing's right you do with Caroline? She's never in the same helement two days together. She's downright contrairy in her temper; and what's a greater consideration for you, she can't taste the curd, and I should like to know what profit a cheese-farmer can make out of such a wife as that! No! you've missed your road, my lad, and you must trace your steps back again.' 'How can I, Mother?' says he.

So after a good bit of reasoning he agreed to follow my counsel; I said to him, 'Now I would not speak on the pint

of the curd if I was you, but I'd tell
Caroline that you're a man as requires a
comfortable partner, and then I'd make a
bit the worst of myself, and tell her what
a bad husband you'd make to any woman
that had an uneasy temper. So the next
day he went over to Hurst, and he said
pretty near all as I told him to Caroline,
and her cried and said her could not alter
her temper for no man. So then he went
to the Mother, and he had a bit of a job
with her at first, for she was not willing
to let him have Jane. She said, 'Mr.
Harland, you was welcome at the first
start to the _chice_ of my daughters, but
now I cannot see Caroline murdered.' So
then George pinted out how murder was
a deal more likely to occur after marriage
if they was unhappy; and somehow he
managed to turn the old lady round (he's

very enticing in conversation, Miss G.), and
so it was agreed he might send messages
to Jane in his sister's letters. But that
did not go on long, for my daughter Mary
is grown very serious, and I rather think
she writes a many *texes* in her letters, and
she decided that the love bits was un-
shuitable. However, things have come
round quite agreeable now, for Caroline
has took up with another lover. Really,
I think there's hardly a lad in all this
country as would have pulled through
such a job so well as our George; but
you see he's very good looking—he has
such nice curling, 'air. Dear me! what a
way he was in because the servant girl
stole his 'air hile just as Jane was coming
here to conclude about being married. He
wanted me to turn the girl off, but I says,
' Where am I to get my pails cleaned if I

must look out for a girl as won't steal
'air hile, its nateral to 'em all; you should
consider they like their 'air to look nice
as well as you.'

1860.

*Miss G., Mrs. Harland, and her daughter
Mary.*

Mrs. H.—Our George was married to
Jane Thornton the same day as Caroline
was married to Joseph Brayford.

Mary H.—Eh! Miss G. Caroline is in
luck's way. I wish many a time I'd lit of
such a man as Joseph Brayford; his
civility's grand, and such a Honorable dis-
position, and milks fifty-three cows.

Mrs. H.—Yes. And do you know, Miss
G., I do believe I caused my son to make

the wrong chice betwixt the two sisters. He'd better have stuck to Caroline, for she's been making two cheeses a day ever since she was married, and I hear them very well spoken of. Now, Jane's cheese, in my judgment, won't hit our Factor's fancy. I said to her when she was first married, 'Jane,' says I, 'the cheeses off our pastures cannot be put together in the same form as they're done on the other side the country, so you had better watch and see how our old Martha does them.' Eh! how I did affront her. 'She wasn't come here to be learnt by a servant indeed.' But the Thorntons have all been brought up to look at servants as beasts of labour. And Jane has hurt my feelings in another way, too, Miss G. You see, I'd put myself about all roads before the wedding to make things comfortable for her at Hallwood. I'd gone there two or three times a day in the heat of the sun with fithers for the beds, and bits of bedside carpets, and macassars for the Parlor chairs, and two or three chaney ornaments as I could spare. Well, and when Jane came she never took notice of nothing —no more than if she'd stepped into a hempty Barn! When Caroline came over to see her, I took her on one side, and I said, 'Caroline, I'm afraid Jane's not content, at least, if she is, she makes no acknowledgment.' 'Mrs. Harland,' said Caroline, 'Jane is a Thornton, and Thorntons never acknowledges nothing.'

Mary H.—I call that all pride and hignorance, indeed pride is hignorance, Miss G., and I consider it's more like a gentleman's wife than a cheese farmer's to sit of a morning in the Parlor, with her hair in a net and bugles, doing embroidery—downright hidle I call it; and it's strange when there's not one hidle bone in us Harlands, that George's wife and Anne's husband should both be so hidle; it's a shame to see Goodman lying on the sofa when Anne's swatting and toiling over the cooking, and then, when he's eat his dinner, he hactually goes and lays him down again, and then, maybe, towards four o'clock, he'll get up and feed the fowls, or at most look for a hegg, or take the children a bit of a walk.

Mrs. H.—and he's something like my daughter-in-law for acknowledging nothing, for do you know, Miss G., that ever since I lent him a fifty pound note he never speaks to me at all. I went in the other day, and there was a leg of lamb roasting—so nothing would serve Anne but I must stop for dinner; and, would you believe me, Goodman never came in to dinner, tho' I know he's particular partial to roast lamb; indeed, I tell Anne she lets him have it a deal too often, for he's a good deal encumbered with flesh.

Mary H.—I often say to mother, if I must be a slave to such a rubbishy harticle as Mr. Goodman (I always call him Mr. to keep him at a distance), I'd rather be Mary Harland to the last.

Mrs. H.—Well, my girl, you are likely enough to be. She gets harder to please every year, Miss G. Now, I told her I'd ask you whether, even amongst real gentlemen, there was many as was altogether perfect?

Miss G.—Many!! O dear! not one.

Mrs. H.—There's for you, Mary! It's sixteen or seventeen letters you've turned back, isn't it?

Mary H.—I can't say for certain. I'll tell you, Miss G., how I serve them. I wish to show them every respect, so I get a right down good envelope—not one of them flimsy things—and I put the gentleman's letter in it with a small bit of paper wrapped round it, with these words, 'Mary Harland is much obliged, but she is engaged.' I used to put 'but she's too young,' before I was turned twenty-one; but one of them wrote again twice, and then I was forced to explain my sentiments. I told him he was High Church (he never misses morning nor evening), and I'd been brought up to the Chapel. I shouldn't mind a bit changing to the church, Miss G., if other things were agreeable, but I couldn't tell him the real cause for laying him o' one side; I'd heard he'd had a touch of the rheumatics two Springs together, and you know, Miss G., a farmer as couldn't go out in all weathers would make but a poor profit.

Mrs. H.—Well, Mary, Miss G. will own that was a good reason; but now tell her why you wouldn't have John Ellison.

Mary H.—Why, Miss G., he is all but a fool, and so boastful and house proud. Mother deserved a good chastising for trying to make me have him.

Mrs. H.—There's not a nicer house in all the county than his, with yew trees cut into forms, and such nice short turf and gravel walks; and he's a pretty looking man, too, and no foolisher than other folks as I can see; to be sure he does come out with foolish things in his talk sometimes, but, Miss G., Mary finds just as much fault with them as don't talk at all.

Mary H.—To be sure I do. I can't put up with a sign-post. I should like to have a man as knows how to put the right word forward in the right place; one as I shouldn't be ashamed of in company. Then it must be allowed that a pious man is the first consideration, though I must own that the one of 'em as I like best is not a bit pious.

Miss G.—Who is it, Mary?

Mary H.—Well, ma'am, if you must know, it is Robert Thornton, Jane's brother. Him with the rheumatics.

1861.

Miss G., Mrs. Harland, and her daughter Mary.

Mrs. H.—We were going to bring my daughter-in-law and the baby to see you, Miss G., only Mary said she couldn't open

2

her mind to you about Robert before his sister.

Mary H.—No, you see, I shouldn't wish to show the inside of my mind to Jane, for I'm as undecided as ever, though I've been partly engaged since last August was a twelvemonth. Robert had paid me a vast of attention for five years, but he never came out and out till then. He said, 'Mary, you and me have been acquainted long enough, and I don't see why we should not get married.' So I says, 'Robert, I cannot say as I've any objections to you, only I've always built myself up that I'd marry a pious man, and a pious man I will have.' 'Well,' says he, 'I'm not pious for certain, but I've always striven to do what is right.' 'Maybe you have,' says I, 'but that's nothing at all to the purpose; I must have a man that has set himself fully to serve the Lord.'

So of course he could not say he had ; but he went on writing the beautifullest of letters, mentioning his soul pretty often ; and just before Christmas he came over, and there was a class meeting ; you know we all as belongs to the class tells one another our experiences ; so after we had done there was a long silence, and then Mr. Green shouted out ever so many times, 'Who'll be on the Lord's side?' and nobody answered—we rather expected my youngest brother to speak, but I suppose he didn't feel fully ripe ; so the preacher bawled out louder than ever, till at last Robert jumped up and shouted, ' I will.' Eh! I was astonished above a bit.

Miss G.—I suppose you were much pleased, Mary ?

Mary H.—I can't say as I was altogether, for I knew I should have to put him off with something else. Accordingly the next morning, Robert came to me as I was skimming, and says, 'Mary, you said you couldn't marry me till I was converted, and now as I've made that all right, I hope you'll give me satisfaction.' 'Robert,' I said, 'I'm glad as you've turned your feet into the right road, and I hope you're sincere, but we've had a heavy make of cheese this year, and mother's arms is getting weak, and I couldn't think of leaving her to turn them ; you had better go and talk it over with mother.' Now, mother, it is you to speak.

Mrs. H.—Well, Miss G., when Robert came to me he was crying and sobbing ever so, I couldn't help but be sorry for him, though I did laugh a bit too ; and when he had got his speech he murmurs out, 'Mrs. Harland, for all I've got converted I'm never a bit forwarder with Mary as I can see.' 'You must have patience, my lad,' says I, 'Mary is not one as can be pushed to a determination ; you must wait till she's got the cheeses off her mind, and then she'll see more about it in the spring.' I only said this to peacify him, you know, so he says, 'Mrs. Harland, I'd wait four or five years more if I could make sure of not being deceived at last, but that's what I'm afeard of.' And poor fellow, he cried so he was actially obliged to stop here till the next day. We must allow he is very awkiardly situated, for spring and summer have gone past since then, and he's just where he was ; Mary's never short of some excuse.

Miss G.—Well, Mary, I think Robert would make you a very kind husband.

Mary H.—I'm not a bit afraid about the

kindness; indeed, I am well aware I should be master, tho' he is a beautiful upstanding man to look at, isn't he, mother?

Mrs. H.—Yes, that he is, and Mary would be as nicely fixed at Green Hayes as anybody could desire, there's such a beautiful big front to the house; to be sure the kitchen comes to the front, but the window looks like a parlour, and there's scenery for scores of miles over the country, and inside there's a tremendious lobby as long as a street. I was stopping two or three days a while ago with Robert, when his father and mother was out, and the evening they was expected home to tea, Robert put the kettle on, and then he set his father's and his mother's slippers before the fire, and I look a deal at his being such a good son; however, his good properties don't seem to satisfy Mary; for one thing she has set her mind on, a family haltar, and she thinks Robert wouldn't be ready at making prayer ; so you see betwixt one thing and another Robert has got a big job before him to bring the matter to a close.

Mary H. (bursting into tears)—Indeed, Miss G., I often think I darena be married, I see so many as are uncomfortable.

1862.

Miss G., Mrs. Harland, and Mary.

Mary H.—I've thought a deal at what you said, Miss G., when we parted, about Robert making a good husband, and a cousin of mine says to me one day, 'Mary, there's happiness for you written on Robert's face.' So at Christmas I told Robert as I was quite agreeable to be married in May if he

was, and of course he said he was; but when
I told mother she seemed so cast down that
next morning, when he came, I says to him,
'Robert, mothers are before husbands, and
I can't go against mother; you must speak
to her.'   Now, mother, you tell Miss G.
about it.

Mrs. H.—Well! I didn't come to the pint
of what my reasons were at wunst, but I
worked it round.   'Robert,' says I, 'it's
very hard usage for parents to be robbed of
their children just when they're most useful,
but young men thinks they must have their
own road in everything; a good wife is a
valyable thing, and you must learn to wait
patiently for one.'   So he says, 'Well, I
wanted to have had Mary five years ago.'
'Yes,' says I, 'you did, Robert, more's the
pity you were so unreasonable, just after the
Lord had taken our poor Sophia, to think as

we could part with another to you, and a
cheese every day, and Hemily only eleven!
It was a small consideration to you as I
must break my back over the cheese-tub.'
'Well,' says he, 'but now Hemily is sixteen,
and a fine tall girl.' 'Yes,' says I, 'she is
tall, you've just hit it, and that's why she is
weakly. She's all legs and arms, besides
she's not perfect in her hedication; I don't
look so much at the piano as at the writing
and casting. There's a deal of mud down
the lane as she goes along to school, and
ever since our Sophia died I've been very
timorsome about Hemily wetting her feet.
She must have another year.' So Robert
was very quiet, for he saw I was as firm as a
rock, and he could not but say as Hemily
must have her hedication, so now we've
settled the wedding for next spring.

1863.

Miss G., Mrs. Harland, and her daughter
Mary, in a house at Bewley. After a
time, Mrs. Brayford comes in.

Mary H.—Eh, dear! Miss G. Mother
and me have been so put about by missing
seeing in the Middleshire paper that Mrs.
Bingham (Miss Clare that was) had a daughter. You see, we were quite lost and con-
founded by the name not being the same as
the gentleman's father's. If we had seen
Mrs. Bridgenorth, we should have been right
enough. They've christened the baby
Georgina, haven't they? And, do you
know, it's the unaccountablest thing in
all the world; but as much as four months
before she was born my brother and
his wife had called their baby Georgina.

I do hope Mrs. Bingham won't take it amiss.

Miss G.—Oh, no. Certainly not. But she will be sorry to hear you are not married yet.

Mary H.—Oh! this marrying, Miss G., it's a harder job than ever. I fully thought it was all coming to a finish last February, for Robert was dangerously ill. I can't say I was not grieved, but I made myself comfortable in this way. You know I've been praying all along to the Lord to interpose with something of a sign; so I thought maybe his death was to be it. He didn't seem quite pleased when I told him how I felt—he hasn't gained that much Faith yet —and he drove me fairly into a corner about getting married in May, till, indeed, we came to have a little unpleasantness.

Mrs. H.—Yes, I was obliged to sit me

down betwixt them, and deliver my mind
first to one and then to the other. 'Mary,' I
said, ' Robert is in a debilitated condition
and he must not be put about.' Then I
spoke quite collected to Robert. 'Robert,'
says I, 'if Mary's not worth waiting for
she's not worth having; young women is
not reared to be given to young men just for
the asking. When May was fixed on, how
could we forecast that Hemily's liver would
be so disranged as to prevent her turning
even the shabbiest sized cheese? and no one
can say as our cheeses are shabby !'

Mary H.—Yes, and then the three weeks'
wash, Miss G. My youngest brother, John,
said to me so pitiful, 'Who'll get up our
collars and shirt-fronts when you are gone?'
I fairly bursted out crying. And there's
another thing that makes me dubious, Miss
G.—Robert's father and mother purposes

living with us for the present   I don't mind
the old gentleman ; he's as tractable as can
be, but *she* is so close and made-up like.

Miss G.—Does she seem fond of you ?

Mary H.—Well, she makes no expression
of it.

Miss G.—Are you afraid of her finding
fault with your housekeeping ?

Mrs. H. (with immense dignity)—Miss G.,
I should be very sorry if my daughter
couldn't housekeep above a match for any
of her daughters.   We know what Thornton
housekeeping is, don't we, Mary ?   I think,
Miss G., that if the old lady takes to count-
ing Mary as one of her own family all will
be right, for Thorntons think there's nothing
like Thorntons.   I will say this, I never saw
married folks as taddled after each other
like this old couple.   When her and me was
going out in the shandery, the old gentle-

man was as careful and solemn as could be,
tucking her cloak round her and managing
her steel, for I could see she wore a pretty
stiff one, though I won't say it was big ; and
then he shambled off to open us the gate.

Mary H.—Robert and me have settled it
now that in September we must close the
matter, hon or hoff. I dare not fix the day,
nor I daren't get any new clothes, for fear I
should run in at the very last. Eh! this
marrying, I'm quite wearied out about it. I
had quite as lief die and have done with it.
You will be glad to hear, ma'am, that
George's wife is a deal humbled since
they've been sold up. She even said to me,
'Your mother has priced us, and flitted us,
and settled us'; that was some acknowledgment, and out of a Thornton's mouth, too.
We left her and Caroline (that's Mrs. Brayford) in the village, and I'll go and fetch

them. (*After their entrance, and some gene-*
ral conversation, Mrs. Harland turned to
Mrs. Brayford)—

Mrs. H.—Now, Caroline, you are well
fixed—for your land is good and your husband is good, though, to be sure, he doesn't
perfess religion, does he?

Mrs. B.—I would rather not say.

Mrs. H.—I daresay; but you wouldn't
be going for to say as he has got his soul ﹅
saved.

Mrs. B.—I don't know anything about it.

Mrs. H.—Why, Caroline! what ever has
come to you? Not know, indeed! Just
as if it was a thing as could be hid. Well,
it is plain, my girl, that you'll never help
him over the stile. Thorntons, Miss G., are
all for this world.

1864.

Miss G. and Mrs. Harland.

Mrs. H.—Though it is a many months since Mary's wedding, it's not over with my sorrowing, Miss G. Our house has never been the same—everything was in the right place when Mary was here. The week before she was married I said I could not go through with it; but my husband and sons were both on Robert's side, and the flys were ordered (and there were seven of them), so I was forced to give way; but I always will keep to it, Miss G., that I am as deserving of my daughter as any gentleman in all England. Before ever Robert took her to the church, I said to him, 'Now, Robert, you go down on your knees and thank me for letting you have her'; and he went down as composed as could be. Mary was married in a bridal fall and wreath that came quite as cheap as a bonnet, and a worked muslin dress that I must own had been washed. She has left that behind for Hemily; but, indeed, I say we can have no more weddings at Bewley; indeed, Hemily is disposed quite the other way, though there are two or three that would be glad to have her, especially since we got such a good price for our cheese. I am happy to say Mary has given the greatest of satis-factions with her cheese at Green Hayes. Before she went away her father said to her, 'Now, Mary, you be sure to do your duty to your cheese, and then you'll put your husband in a persition that he cannot deny you anything in reason that'll make you comfortable.' When I had put my daughter into the fly (they had a pair of white horses) I felt she had set out on the journey of

life away from me, and I could not do with
my husband's trying to pass it off with bits
of jokes, such as ' Mother' (that's me) ' looks
the most stylish of the party,' Miss G.
Mary had a cross laid before the door of
her new house ; the old lady, you see, is a
bit given to drink, and old Mr. Thornton
has been obliged to spend four pounds for a
partition in the lobby, so that Mary's visitors
shan't catch sight of the old lady when she
is unsettled.

A VILLAGE GOSSIP.

1863.

Miss G. and Miss Jackson, sitting in a pretty parlour looking on the village street.

Miss J.—I've been visiting some friends near Norton, and I heard say as Mr. Bingham was a beautiful fellow in the church, and as for Mrs. Bingham, they could not praise her enough ; it made the tears come into my eyes when I thought how we had missed having her at Bewley. Really the rule of contrairy is what marriages go by. I went all over of a tremble the other day when that queer, sheep-faced Mr. John as we always call him, walked into our parlour and said, ' I'm tired of folks talking, so I'm going to be married.' ' Well, Mr. John,' I said, ' I wonder how much

younger you are than when you told me
three or four years ago as you was getting
too old to think of marrying. So he grinned
in his way, and said, 'But you've not guessed
the lady.' 'Well, it never is Miss Long,
surely.' 'Why not?' says he; 'we've been
courting these nineteen years.' Why, Miss
G., it has been every bit on her side, and Mr.
John has told me scores of times in this very
parlour he'd have none of her. Why, he was
wild for years after Miss Caroline C., follow-
ing her up and down like a little dog as was
hunting, and all Miss Long used to say to it
was, ' I can wait a bit longer; I shall have him
at last.' Then when Mr. John got engaged
to his cousin Winifred, Miss Long said
quite cool, 'O! she'll die consumptive before
they can get married, and then I shall have
him,' and sure enough it's all come true;
really, it's like something out of a book.

Did Miss Smith tell you about a lady as lodged with her a whole year and nobody ever could find out who she was, nor what she was, nor where she came from? and Bewley is not behind many places for prying. She never went out except at night, and mostly sat with her room door locked. Miss Smith says she's positive she was a real born lady, for she hadn't the least hidea how to do hanything for herself; it took her hours to peel her potatoes. Once Miss Smith did just look through the keyhole, and she was on her knees, but Miss Smith wouldn't say for certain whether she was at her prayers or washing some of her clothes out. Once she went out on a visit for a week, and then Miss Smith thought she should have a chance of seeing the directions on her box, but there was none put on it. Miss Mason went in Mrs. Malpas's gig, and the boy who drove her to the station told his Missis that he watched her take a card out of her pocket, and tie it on her box as the train came up; downright crafty I call that. Then nobody ever saw the postman give her a letter, and as she used to walk to Southwick now and then, we rather think her letters were left at the Southwick post-office, at any rate none passed through this post-office, for I got that out of Mrs. Palmer after Miss Mason was gone for good. I never saw her close but once, and then I made an excuse to go and borrow a cream jug off her. I knocked over and over at the door, and then she opened it an inch or two, and when she saw it was me, she banged the door in my face, and locked it, just as if I'd been a burglar. She had been either a felon or a lunatic herself, I'm positive.

BETTY WEST AND HER PIG.

1845.

*Miss G. and Betty West, a Labourer's wife,
in a cottage.*

Betty W.—Eh! dear, ma'am, we've lit of
such a bad misfortin; we'd pinched and
pinched all as ever we could to buy a pig;
so on Monday James and me gets up at
four o'clock and walks to Oldcastle, and
we picks out the nicest lookingst as ever
you saw, and we give thirty shillings for
him, and sets out home as pleased as could
be. Well, ma'am, we hadn't got much past
half-way when I says to James, 'I say, I
dunnot like the way as yon pig drags his
legs after him.' 'Hold thy noise, woman,'
says he; 'pig's right enough.' James has

a bit of a hot temper, you know, ma'am, but it's soon off him again. Well, so we goes another mile, and then I says to James, 'James, I'm sartain sure that pig is bad, say what you will.' So then he turned round quite sharp, and says, 'There's always death and destruction in thy mouth, woman.' You know, ma'am, he see'd as pig was bad, just as well as me, and finely put about he was. Eh! dear, what a way he was in, to be sure! You know, ma'am, it was as though he was striving all as ever he could to lay the fault on me, and he kept on saying, 'There's niver no pleasure nor profit in nothing when women's consarned.' So I holds my tongue, for you know, Miss G., when men's a thattens, it's no use aggravating of 'em.

A SICK MAN.

Miss G., Samuel Shaw, a poor and sick man, and his wife, sitting together over the fire.

Samuel.—Miss G., I want to speak to you about my money in your savings-bank. You see, ma'am, I should like it to be tied up, so as if I died this woman here shouldn't go and squander it away with some scampering young chap or other.

Miss G.—Oh, Samuel! how can you think of Martha doing such a thing?

Martha.—Never mind, ma'am. Let him tie his money which way he likes. You may depend I've had enough of marrying. I shall never put my head into that yoke never no more. Only see how my poor legs is swelled with running up and down stairs of a night, to get him things when he can't sleep for coughing. I've had enough of marrying.

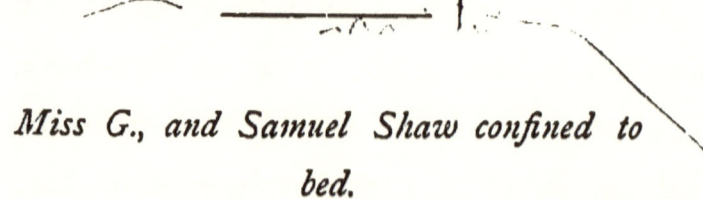

Miss G., and Samuel Shaw confined to bed.

Samuel.—Well, ma'am, I'm very bad to-day, for I've been sadly put about. This morning, just before dinner-time, I hears somebody open the house door, and then he comes to the foot of the stairs and shouts out, 'Well! Samuel, how are you this morning?' So then I knowed as it was Mr. Harland, the preacher. So I says, 'Thank you, sir; I gets weaker and worse every day.' So he shouts out again, as loud as ever he could, 'That's not what I want to know. I mean whether you've got your soul saved yet?'

Miss G.—That was a very hard question to answer: tell me what you said.

Samuel.—Well! ma'am, I was sadly put about, and I could scarce speak for coughing, but after a bit I says, 'Well, sir, I prays to the Lord night and day, and I hopes He'll forgive me afore He taks me.'

Miss G.—A very proper answer; and what did Mr. Harland say?

Samuel.—Why, if you'll believe me, ma'am, he flew into the biggest passion as ever was, and he shouts out as loud as ever he could, 'Your soul will be lost to all eternity, for those very words you've just spoken. What's the use of you bothering the Lord with them prayers of yours. I suppose you expect to see Him come into

the room with a pair of wings. Don't
you know that He is waiting at your
bedside now, to save your soul, only you
won't let Him?'

———————

AN ASTROLOGER.

1845.

Miss G. and Mrs. Raikes, the Gardener's wife.

Miss G.—You seem low; has Raikes been drinking again?

Mrs. R.—Don't ask me about it, please, ma'am.

Miss G.—Why not?

Mrs. R.—Because, if I was to tell you, he would find me out in a minute by them nasty stars.

Miss G.—What can you mean?

Mrs. R.—Well, ma'am, you know he's always a reading in those big books of his about the stars, and then he casses folks' nativities. Eh! dear ma'am, you would laugh to see how the girls out of the village comes creeping in here of a night to ask Raikes about their sweethearts. They pretends to ask if he's got any apples to sell, or such like; but I knows very well what they're after, so I takes no notice, but says quite careless, 'You can go into the parlour to Raikes'; so then they sneaks in, and I can hear plenty of whispering—but I am never that false to listen, you know, ma'am —and when the girls come out again some on 'em looks fine and vexed, you may depend. It's plain enough when he's been telling them their sweethearts won't have 'em.

Miss G.—It is very foolish of them; but I think it is very wrong of Raikes.

Mrs. R.—Oh! but you know, ma'am, it's all attending the Scriptures; he always charges his glasses with a text before he looks in.

Miss G.—How has Raikes's temper been lately?

Mrs. R.—Not a bit better, only I've left off 'taliating with him ever since he knocked a jug of new milk off the table and broke it. You see, Miss G., all men has their tempers, only some'll bear 'taliating with and some won't. Now, there's Joseph, my sister's husband, he's as nasty stupid a temper as need to be; but Mary always 'taliates with him, and then he's as meek as a lamb in a minute. She often says to me, 'Sarah, why don't you 'taliate with Raikes?' Why, dear me, Miss G., Raikes 'ud break every bone in my body if I did. However, I'd a deal rather have him, with all his tempers, than such a fandawdling husband as Mr. Downes. Why, he'd lay his hands on the ground for his wife to walk over! For my part, I hates them soft fellers.

Miss G.—I am sure you will be glad to hear that Mrs. Baddiley had a son born yesterday.

Mrs. R.—That is good news indeed!

Miss G.—Why did you turn round and look at the clock?

Mrs. R.—Why, you see, ma'am, whenever I tell Raikes of a child being born, he always asks me, 'What o'clock was it?' and he's very cross if I can't tell him, and you know I can scarce ever say for certain what o'clock it was when a child was born; so now I always say what o'clock it was when first I heard tell of it.

——— ———

MARY KING.

1857.

Miss G. and Mary King, a Labourer's wife, sitting together in Mary's cottage.

Miss G.—How have you and John agreed together since I left Bewley?

Mary.—Well, ma'am, those words of yours when we parted have hacted very well. 'Mary,' says you, 'when John's in a bad temper you be in a good 'un; for it's both on you being in a bad temper together as does the mischief.' So mony a time when he's contraried me I've said to myself, 'Now I'll be on Miss G.'s plan'; and we've had nothing but bits of houts since— never no fighting—and a very good thing

4

we've left it hoff. For, ye see, a man's hand falls very heavy on a woman, and mony a time I've been black and blue; only he was a deal more careful where he hit me at after he had that seven-and-six-pence to pay for them leeches to my side. You remember it; don't you, ma'am? I'd been saying summat again his mother—he calls her all to pieces himself, only he wunna let me—so he knocked me hoff the chair, and it caused himplamation; and fine and foolish John looked when the doctor shook his head at him. But he niver said he was sorry; he's too stupid for that.

Miss G.—Have you taken my advice on the other point—about going to church?

Mary.—Well, ma'am, I did go twice after my brother died; but I can scarce ever find time, betwixt waiting on the cow, and the pig, and John—and he taks as much as

t'other two put together ; he won't so much
as reach out his hand to reach hisself a cup
or a saucer. I gets up at four o'clock on
Sundays to milk cow, and then there's
John's boots to be blacked, and a deal of
mud scraped off 'em first, and breakfast to
get in time for him to go to chapel at nine
(and he scolds me finely if he's late), and
then pig to be fed and our dinner to get. I
said to John one Sunday, when he'd been
saying, 'Woman, thou'lt go to Fire and
Brimstone as sure as thou'rt born, for thou
niver goest to church nor chapel'; 'Very well,'
says I, 'then thou must feed pig thyself
to-day.' 'I'll let him starve first,' says
John ; and, sure enough, pig would have
starved if I had na' crep out at night to feed
him. So when I come back I thought I'd
have it out wi' John, so I says, 'I'm not a
bit likelier to go to Fire and Brimstone than

thou art, with all thy blaating and praying ;
and as for them Methodies, I hates 'em,
with all them collections, sixpence here and
sixpence there, and I have read in a book
that John Wesley did not improve of their
axing folks for money.' So John says quite
scornful, ' I wonder where you got that
much larning, woman.' 'When I had the
hopportunity,' I says quite scornful back
again. You know, Miss G., I'd read it in a
book as was full of all manner of things
about railroads and such like. I suppose
ma'am, you've seen London Bridge. Eh !
dear, what a place it must be ! they say the
railway carriages, and carriages and cabs
with horses, are all running together upon
the rails, and it's nothing but them pints as
keeps them from all being smashed together.

1859.

Miss G. and Mary King.

Miss G.—How have you and John been getting on since I saw you?

Mary K.—Pretty well; indeed, I darsna fly into them passions; the doctor says it'll be present death if I do. Mine is the white passions as drives the blood hinwards and causes bad palpulation at the heart. Mr. Walker, the doctor, come in one day just as I'd knocked John back'ards at the door for coming in with dirty shoes just when I'd been two hours on my hands and knees' cleaning the floor; but you know, Miss G., a hot temper is naterally grounded in me. My mother had a hawful temper; I've seen her empty a shovel full of hot ashes on my father's head. Now, I won't

say but what I've thrown a ash or two at
John, but they've been could 'uns ; and one
day my mother snatched up a gown as I
had been buying for myself, and put it on
the fire, and her said, 'There now, and next
time I'll put you on the fire too, if you buy
finery without my jurydiction.' Eh! how I
cried 'when I see'd them beautiful pink and
yallow stripes kindling ; but her was a good
mother at the root for all her was so strict ;
and when I sees girls nowadays fithered and
flounced up, and pomped out so as when
they comes swelling along one's obliged to
get out o' the road, I often thinks to myself,
it's a pity there's not some mothers in
Bewley like mine. John often says to me,
'Thou'rt the very model of thy mother,
Mary, temper and all.' 'Yes, John,' says I,
'and didn't her warn thee that I'd a foul
temper ; and didn't thee say, like a big fool,

"I wull have her, temper and all." Thou
conceitedst thou couldst master me, but
thou hast larnt different.' 'I have that,'
said John. He often fetches texes out
of Scripture about women doing their
juties, to clench me with, and he knows it
taks me a long time to pick out a tex to
clinch him with. There was no natteral
schools whin I was yong. John was very
near 'ticing me to chapel t'other Sunday to
hear a round preacher, only my clothes is
rather shabby, and now I'm poorly I dunna
like to buy new 'uns, for fear other folks
should get 'em after I'm jead; so I didna
go, and when John come home I axed him
what benefit he'd got, and he said, 'Not so
much as usual.' So then, after jawing with
him a good bit to tell me, I drawed it out of
him as the Preacher had said, 'If you don't
all come to me after service and confess

every bit of sin, you'll be jead in three hours.' So I said to John, 'It's right down lucky I didn't go to chapel, for I'm sartain sure I should have got up and pulled him out of the pilpit.' 'I'll be bund thou wouldst, woman,' says John ; and then I says, 'If I was you, John, I should be ashamed to go to listen to such folks ; but I verily think thou'dst go to hear the Devil himself if he did but bawl loud enough.' I hates them Methodies, Miss G.; but still old William Smith made a fine finish of it, and was buried, too, very respectable, with hatbands at five-and-sixpence a yard, and funeral cards with hurns and willers.—I'm thinking of getting mine framed against the wall.

1860.

Miss G. and Mary King.

Miss G.—As you always say the cow pre-
vents your going to church, I think you had
better give up keeping one.

Mary K.—Why, Miss G., you don't consider as the flour, and tea, and sugar, and a
bit of beef now and then of a Sunday, and
John's thick boots, all comes out o' the cow.

Miss G.—Surely John's wages might do
all that.

Mary K.—Dear-a-me! Miss G., ten shillings a week goes no way at all again the
rent and firing's taken out of it. You're
partly the same as John was, when we was
first married; our biggest fallings out was
because he thought the money had ought to
go iver so much further till it would. He
expected as a pund o' sugar and a quarter

o' tea 'ud last us six months, and he'd always swallowed down two cups o' tea afore I could get my one poured out. I've skinned my poor feet scores o' times walking to Oldcastle to get things a halfpenny cheaper, because he abused me so about the money. There's no black in all Africay as has been a bigger slave till me, I'm sartain sure. However, I can see the hend coming some day as I shall get hease, and, as I often tells John, when I get shut of him I'll tak care how I'm tied to another.

Miss G.—Oh! Mary, I am sure that if John were to die before I come to see you again, you would be crying sadly, and telling me what a loss you had had.

Mary K.—Maybe I should. You know me pretty well, ma'am; but for all that, rough words and hard work wull harden anybody's heart as well as their fingers.

It is very haggravayting to hear other folks
tell as how their husbands peels the 'taters
and gets tea when they're a washing.   I
never axed John to get tea but wunst, and
then he sets the cups and saucers all of a
ruck on a chair where one might have sat
down upon 'em ; and then if he didna let
the kettle fall back'ards into the fire and
put it out.   Mary Harrison come in one
day last week, and her was bragging that
Samuel got up of a Sunday morning and lit
the fire, and milked cow, and cleaned shoes
afore her and Hemily was up, and her says,
'If I was you, Mary King, I'd mak John do
the same for you.'   So says I, 'John was
never brocken to such work when he was a
lad'; and you know, ma'am, men's just like
the young things—calves—that one rares,
they must be brocken.   But I'll tell you what,
Miss G., I will go to church as soon as we

can light of a bit of a croft as isn't so far
down the common lane. You know where
ours is now ; it's towards that house where
the Methodies has their prayer meetings ;
and as them and me goes down the lane
together they often slaps it in my face as I
shall go to Fire and Brimstone—just as if
shouting and skriking 'ud tak folks to
Heaven. Why, I can hear 'em bawling
when I'm milking cow ; and I'll assure
you, Miss G., cow stares and shakes her
head ever so ; and if the dumb animals taks
such notice at the nise, you may judge what
hold it taks of Christians ; but in t'other
croft cow and me shall be shut of their
bawling, and I shall have time to run home
after church and doff my Sunday clothes.
I couldna for shame go to church in my
milking cloak ; you know, it was that as
made Parson Taylor axe if I was a Hirish-

woman. I shall never forgive him for them words; maybe I should if I'd iver had a chance to give it him back again. I watch'd my hopportunity sharp enough, but I niver cotched him. Think of a parson calling a decent woman by such titles!

Miss G.—To return to the church-going question; I wish people would not always think it necessary to put their best clothes on for church.

Mary K.—Best clothes! Why, I should be more ashamed o' going to church in my best clothes till in my milking cloak. Folks would pint at me going up th' aisle in a silk gown! I've niver had my best clothes on but wunst in all the seventeen years I've been married, and that was when I went to the Collieries to see Mrs. Benson. I'd a bonnet with white ribbins, and a black silk gown as was given to my mother afore her

was married, and a brown cloth mantle ; the
moths got into that four or five years back,
so I was forced to cut it into a waiscoat for
John ; but it was as handsome a thing as
need be seen then, and you may judge it
was, for as I rounded the corner by Wilson's
field I came right again Thomas Whitmore,
and what does he do but doff his hat and
mak me a boo. You see, Miss G., he hactially
took me for a lady of some kind. I felt fine
and foolish, and eh! how Thomas stared
when I bust out laughing and he see'd it
was me ; you know I could see plain enough
he was finely vexed at having booed to such
a one as me, so I says, 'Well, Thomas,
there's no occagin to begrudge me the boo,
I shall never ax thee for another, and it's
done thee no harm as I can persheive.' So
then he laughed, and he said, 'Well, woman,
thou may'st keep the boo.'

1861.

Miss G. and Mary King.

Mary K.—I hope you're better of the lombagger, Miss G. John had it wunst, and he was cured with some stuff he got gracious from Doctor Woods; it was uncommon strong, for he could feel it playing back'ards and forrards about his heart afore it went down. John's mother is dead at last, but she lay a long while; you know sick folks canna go hoff unless they're kept nice and clean; I'll be bound her'd have died a deal sooner if I'd had the tending of her, because I should always have been fettling and washing of her. For all her'd been so wicked, her died like a good 'un, and said her was going to Glory; but I'm partly of your opinyan, Miss G., that according as

folks live, so they'll die. You know we've
hall talents as must be fulfilled, and it's
no use skriking and bawling like them
Methodies ; you know they're all thrutched
up in a little room till they're as hot as iver
they can be, and then they says it's the
power of the Lord as is come upon 'em, and
the women throws off their bonnets, and
shouts, 'Glory! Glory!' But I've took a
resolution as I'll go to church of an after-
noon, as soon as we're settled in the new
house, but I do believe as folks cannot sit
comfortable in the pews for them crenolines.
They'll not come often alongside o' me in
'em, I warrant 'em, for I'll take a knife with
me, and I'll let 'em hout. I wish as I'd
some o' their wide gowns to make bed
curtains, and I tells 'em so too, for I am not
one as laps up my speech—it comes straight
out. It is na' the best folks as dresses finest.

As Miss Lawton stood at our window yesterday, her cries out to me, 'Why, who iver can
that be going along the road? Her canna
for sure be one of the ladies—her's dressed
so oncommon plain.' So I jumps up, and
who should it be but Miss Harriet? So I
says, 'Well, her is remarkable plain, sure
enough, no flounces, nor cross pieces, nor
nothing; but,' I says, 'our ladies are not like
some as puts all their money on their backs
—their sarvants taks half their money, I
know—but I warrant if you went close up
and felt at Miss Harriet's gown it 'ud be
nice and thick, none of your flimsy rubbishy
harticles.'

1864.

Miss G. and Mary King.

Mary K.—Eh! dear, Miss G., when I heard tell of Mr. Briggs's murder, I went all of a tremble, and I says to John, 'We shall be sure to be having our ladies murdered some day, for they're always going about on them railroads.' So John says, 'Dunnot myther thyself o' thattens about them; do ye think our ladies are such simples as they canna tak care o' themselves? I'll be bund they niver gets into a coach where there's a man, they rides with the women and childer.' I shall niver forget the night as the farm-house where I lived sarvant was attacted by house-breakers. One night, when we was sitting at work in the house-place, I felled like as if my eyes was drawed to a space as there was

'twixt the shutters and the window top, and
there I see'd a man's face, and when I
skriked out to the Missis, and told her what
I seed, 'Thou silly wench,' her said, 'it was
nought but the moon and thy own conceits.'
So I never said no more, for I'm sullen
tempered. But a fortnight afterwards, when
the babby was bad and awake all night with
his teeth, I said to the Missis, 'You'll go to
a skileton with little Johnny and his teething; do let me pester with him to-night.'
So she said as I might; and I said to myself,
'If the thieves come to-night, a teething
babby's as good as a watch dog.' And
sure enough, after twelve o'clock I heard a
nise, and I got up and opened the cage-
ment window, and I heerd a man's voice
say, 'If we canna get the door open we
must tak out a winder pane.' So then I
crep down to the master's and wakened him,

and he says quite cool, ' Strike a light and give me my blunderbush, and then go waken the boys, and tell 'em to bring their blunderbushes.' So I did, and my temper was that stirred that I'm sure if it had not been for the babby I should have gone for a carving knife to stob 'em with. I went back to the garret, and I could hear the master open the house door and cry out, ' Now, boys, shoot away, right and left.' And so they did; but there was nothing hit but the walls and the trees; the shots made a hawful rattling, and there was a deal of good lead wasted, you may depend; but it sarved to let thieves know they'd better not meddle with a house with three blunderbushes in it.

ANNE BERRISFORD.

1863.

Miss G. and Anne Berrisford, a Labourer's wife.

Anne B.—Have you remembered to bring us your——? I can't say long words correct since I've lost my teeth, but it's something that means a poretraite. It wouldn't be paying you proper respect if I was to tell you all that Daniel and me has talked about it, but you won't be offended if I tell you what Daniel said this morning; 'Anne,' says he, 'ax her to let us have her in the full, and not in the side.' You know, ma'am, we thinks it'll look so much liker you yourself, when you're dead and gone. I'm sure, Miss G., I never part with you but what I think I shall never see you again, you are so sickly looking; and there's your sister Miss M., who'd have thought to see her come back alive from foreign parts? But the Lord can do great wonders!

Miss G.—I think you seem as cheerful as ever.

Anne B.—Yes! as Mary Brooks says, I'm always at the top o' the tree, and so I ought to be, for the Lord has been very good to me. You would not have conceited as He would listen to the prayers of a poor hignorant woman like me, but I've pruven as He did; for many a time as my husband has rampaged out of the house door like a lion, I've felled on my knees, and he's come back like a lamb. I never used to tell him what it was as had peacified him, because I knew that 'ud cause him to break out worse till ever; and now when he's a bit for wrangling, I only just say, 'Daniel, we wasn't paired to tear up one another's minds, but to live comfortable.' What sort of a gentleman's temper has Miss Clare that was, got? for I hangs a deal upon folks's tempers. I was so proud to hear of her baby being born into your house; she was the very same as a cade lamb to you and Miss Harriet, and you'd have werrited yourselves to death if she'd been away from you. I should like you to see my youngest girl; she's not out o' the way handsome, for you know, ma'am, I'm hard-featured, and Daniel is long-featured (though he looks pretty well when he's tidied up a bit), but she has the loveliest tongue for a child of two and a half as ever anybody heard. Whatever we say, long or short, she has it in a minute, and specially if there's a bad word said she's sure not to miss it; and then, if I hoffer

to beat her, her'll cry out, 'If mother beats
Hemma, Hemma'll tell daddy, and then
daddy'll beat mother'; really I say such
an admyrable little creatur is more than
nateral. I shall be taking her with me
to chapel by-and-bye; we attends the
Primities.

Miss G.—Are those the Ranters?

Anne B.—Oh! no, ma'am, the Ranters
jump, and the Primities only shouts.   I
don't hold with jumping myself, though to
be sure wasn't it St. Paul—oh, no, it was
King David—as danced before the ark?   The
shouting is a realality, depend upon it, Miss
G., for you know when the facts of the
Lord works into one's inside one cannot
help but shout.

1864.

Miss G. and Anne Berrisford.

Anne B.—I'm very glad you've brought us your likeness, ma'am, for Asher and me often said if you left it us in your will, may be the lawyers would not let us have it, they're so naggling over wills.

That nice-dressed young man with a chain to his watch as you saw into our house is my step-daughter's husband, and for all he is so well off, he equals with us, and scorns neither our bed nor board ; Elizabeth is quite deserving of him, she is so nice looking. Indeed before she married, she was companioned by a lady in Macclesfield, and I think you would almost say to look at her as she was fit to eat with a lady or ride with a lady. I don't say as money is everything in this world, but still on, poor folks has a deal to grattle with; to be sure the rich must grattle with sickness, but ladies may sit with their hands before them if they're a bit poorly; then I take it for the most part ladies' husbands are not so race-brained as poor men.

Miss G.—What does that mean?

Anne B.—I ax your pardon, ma'am, but it means hot-tempered; I'm given to use words as isn't fit to be spoken to a lady, but I was brought up so rough and hignorant that I'm sure it is very good of such 'un as you to speak to me at all.

Oh, yes, I'll send Hemily to school, though I know it will make her strive more than ever after them crinolines; you wouldn't believe how clever she is at rounding out a bit of stick to put under her frock; but it's born with them girls.

DINAH LINDOP. .

Miss G. and Dinah Lindop.

Dinah L.—I suppose, ma'am, you've heard as Anne Wood is gone off with a tramp; her's sould all her husband's chesses of drawers and fither-beds and moggany tables, to get money for her journey. Eh! I've been sadly put about consarning it; her came in here the day afore her went; her and me was always very good friends, so I says to her, 'Anne,' says I, 'how can you for shame let that poor ould man of yours come out of the 'Sylum and find you and his chesses of drawers and fither-beds all gone! and I tell you what, Anne,' says I, 'there's no occagin for you to talk of going to 'Merika, for do you think any ship could

float with such a one as you aboard? No,
your body would soon be at the bottom of the
sea, to be eat up by the fishes, and your soul
in hell fire.' Eh! dear, how her did cry, poor
thing; her and me was always very good
friends; I dar say I frightened her above a
bit, and I knowed her wouldn't dar go to
'Merika, and her didn't.

Betsey Weaver's got very proud sinst her
was married. Eh! dear! how the neebours
all laughed last Sunday when they seed her
and him walking down the lane link and
link. I said to Tummus, 'Thou'd niver for
shame walk with me that fashion;' and he
laughed and said, 'No, wench, that I would
na, not without I was lame or summat.'

MRS. WARD.

Miss G., another Lady, and Mrs. Ward, in a nice cottage in Peakshire.

Mrs. Ward.—I'm very poorly, ladies; the doctor says I've got a skin on my longs, and I'm troubled with them nightly presspirations; they come through nervousness, I think. You see, my husband is sadly given to rambling in his head; he can't sleep for the feelings of his thoughts, and it's very awkard for me, ladies, when I've been toiling and moiling all day, to be kept awake all night discoursing about savation, and nonsensiclar things too; for John says, sometimes, ' I'm going to die, and then thou'lt be sure to be marrying again, for thou'st handsomer every day.' Did you ever

know such conceit, ladies, and me nigh sixty
years old ?   It's all come through that catas-
tropy as befell my husband with a crowbar
(maybe, ladies, you're not apprehensive what
a crowbar is), and when the wound in his
hand was nigh as deep as a well, the doctor
neglected to give him the medicine shutable
for distracting the implimation away from his
head ; but I don't wish to blame the doctor
neither, for he's as tender-hearted a gentleman
as need to be ; he left off being a surgeon
because he could not bear to notomize dead
folks ; he didn't so much mind the men, but
he said it always turned him sick to notomize
a female.   I'm expecting my daughter and
her husband from Australia ; they've been
gone six years, and they'd four children there
and they all died, so as it cost them £3
when they was born, and £6 more when
they was buried, Charles made his calkilations

as that would take away his profits. You see, ladies, luck isn't laid before everybody in this world, but them as has gotten it, always thinks other folks might do as well if it wasn't their own faults. Good-bye, ma'am, you'll be going home to your own family soon?

Miss G.—I'm going home to my sister.

Mrs. Ward.—O! then you're not married! Dear o me! Well to be sure! You'll excuse me for saying so, but I'm particular glad you're not. I've wished scores of times that I'd concluded not to be married myself.

Miss G.—It's the conclusion very few people arrive at.

Mrs. Ward.—Excuse me, ma'am, but you're in a herror. There are two sisters and a brother at Rowland and two brothers and a sister at Broadstone as have all concluded never to be married.

THE STONEMASON.

Miss G. and another Lady, and Mrs. Heath-
cote and her husband, a stonemason.

Mrs. H.—If I'd known it was you,
ladies, I'd have come to the door, but
yesterday there come a knock, and before
I could get to the door it opened, and there
come in, eh! such a length of black fithers
I was fairly frighted; it was some lady in
a hat as had lost her road. My husband
is very bad indeed, ladies; indeed, I thought
it was a done job with him last week, and
him unconvarted yet. He was very near
getting his convarsion last winter; he came
in from the public one Saturday night near
ten o'clock, and he says to me, 'Anne,
it's plain enough thy prayers isn't strong

enough for me, and I'm determined to try what they can do for me at Cresbrook Chapel, and we'll set out this very night, to be ready for the meeting in the morning.' So we set out, and as we passed the Nag's Head I could hear him saying, 'Be off with ye,'—that was to the Devil, you know, ladies. It was twelve o'clock when we got to Cresbrook to my mother's; and as soon as morning came my husband said, 'I'll go to cousin Jane, as has axed me so often to go to chapel, and if her axes me again I'll go.' So he went, but her never axed him, so I took it that the Lord had not appinted this time for Ned, so we come home again, and he soon took to drink worse than ever; but he's better to me than he used to be, for when I knelt down to say my prayers he'd often pull me up again by the roots of my hair. He's coming down stairs now,

6

ladies. 'Ned, thou must tell these ladies what ails thee, though they'll maybe scarce understand such broad talk as thine, but thou must speak thy best and they'll excuse it.'

Edward H.—The doctor says the muscles of my liver is set fast, and he ordered me a hot slivver bath to loosen 'em; so I borrowed one, and while I was in it two or three of the neighbours looked in, and they kept saying, 'Stop in a bit longer, lad, it'll fatch the grease out of thy boones'; so I stopped and stopped till I was well-nigh jead, and I have been going worse ever since.

Miss G.—Have you been subject to these attacks before?

Edward H.—Yes, ma'am, since I was a lad. I was 'prentice to my uncle, a ston-mason, and one day when I was at the top of a ladder, thirty feet high, me and the big ston I was carrying come down together;

and when I laid on the ground half stunned, the first words my uncle said was, 'The ston's not brocken'; he never axed me if I was hurt, and as soon as I could move, he said, 'Up with it again, lad,' so I went, but afore I was half-way up I fainted right away, and fell to the ground with the ston atop of me that time, and I was in bed eleven weeks. My uncle was a bit of a rogue, but he grew to be quite a big sort of a man afterwards, and used to ax me to dinner, and very handsome victuals he set before me, but I niver felt right in the stomach till I'd said summat about the big ston. However, I niver said much, for I kept thinking to myself, 'the words as one has not yet spocken, one has got yet for to say.'

A CLEVER PONY.

Miss G. and Thomas Williams, who was nearly blind.

Miss G.—I am sorry to see your eyes in such a bad state.

Thomas W.—Yes, ma'am, I've had some stuff to burn the disorder out of my eyes, but sometimes my eyes licks the drops, and sometimes the drops licks my eyes.

Miss G.—I hear you have a clever pony that you are fond of her.

Thomas W.—Yes! bless her! her's as much sense as a Christian, and her is as good as a pair of eyes to me; her has saved my life many a time at the railway crossings. Her knows I can't see the trains, and I reckon her ears are sharper than mine, too, for her'll stand as still as a mouse, and then if I kick her to go on her'll snort and stamp her foot, as much as to say, 'Canna ye hear the train, you old fool?' Her's very curious in her temper, and her was the biggest vixen to be brocken as ever I put a halter on. I'll tell you how I brock her: I tied a monument of straw on her back, a thing just like one of us, you know, wi' legs and arms, and I never took it off till her had nigh kicked herself to pieces; but after that I set as many little lads on her as reached from her head to her tail, and her never hoffered to kick 'em off, because you see her thought they was all tied fast on like the monument. Her's very dainty in her eating; you'd laugh to see her pass on a lock of hay as her doesn't quite fancy to the cow as stands alongside of her, as much as to say, 'It's good enough for you.' But her and the cow is good friends, and her was finely put about one day when cow was lost, and a fine piece of work her and me had to find her. Pony was desaved wunst with a cow of Johnson's as had spots same as ours, and her turned off in a fine pet when her got near, and saw it was na ours, and when her did o'ertake cow, pony bumped her head again her a many times, as much as to say, ' D'ye see what a swat I've put myself into to find you, you old stupid.' But I'll tell you what makes me so fond on her; her's the only creatur on this earth as sides wi' me, her and me we fights the world together like. Now my wife cannot side wi' me, for she's one as goes through the world laughing, and I goes through it crying.

Miss G.—I'm afraid your children go through it crying, for I hear you often beat them sadly.

Thomas W.—I does it to larn them to
fight the world ; and besides, since Providence
was so onkind as to take my eyesight from
me, if I wasn't to lay about me with cart whip,
and to cuss and swear hawful at the childer,
they'd be under the wheels every time pony
and me starts in the cart. My mother larnt
me to fight the world sin' I was nine year
old ; I was put to work at a farmer's hard by
our house, and I used to run home crying to
my mother afore daylight, in the snow and
frost, wi' my hands all bleeding wi' handling
the cowld iron of the osses 'arness, and her
used to call me a Molly, and say, ' Niver
mind, lad, blood 'ull toughen thy skin into
lither in a few more bleedings, and then
thou'llt feel nowt.' Her was a right sort of
a woman, and if my wife had tacken pattern
by her, our little Tommy wouldna have been
lying in the churchyard. Her was allus a

giving him what he cried for, and one day he cried for a lighted stick, and burnt hisself to death. And please tak notice of this, ma'am, for all I had chastised him sevarely scores o' times, and the mother was allus a humouring of him, the little feller (God bless him), when he lay a dying, was allays crying out to father instead of mother, cause he was that cute to see as I could turn him and help him best. The mother was dazed like, and afeard to touch him. Yes! I've had a sight of trouble since I got tied to my wife, and I niver should have got tied, only one neebour and another kept saying, 'Why, Ann's none foolisher than the rest of the women in the parish,' and I reckon her is'nt.

———

MARTHA JONES.

Miss G. and Martha Jones, a poor old widow at Llansevern.

Miss G.—Well, Martha, have you had the soup from the Castle yet? Mr. Clare had your name put down for it.

Martha J.—Sure enough I've had it, ma'am; and dear-a-me! it is the beautifullest soup as I ever see. There's pieces of fat that long in it. Indeed, when I looks at 'em those words of the Psalmist do trobble me, 'The wicked do florish.'

Miss G.—I think you need not fear, Martha. You have not flourished much in this world. Shall I tell Mr. Clare how pleased you are?

Martha J.—Oh, yes, God bless him! What a gintleman he's been to me; and him raired the same as the Earl of Clare-mount! And then to think of them Bap-tists speaking so light of him! As I says to them, 'Do you think *I* don't know what a good man is? Me that's been a soldier's wife, and had one child at Bristol and another beyont!' But, for all Mr. Clare's such a grand preacher, I could not abide that sarmon when he spoke so well of marriage. Thinks I to myself, 'Now he'll set all the folks a-marrying'; and sure enough, the next Sunday, what a lot of askings there was! I thought Mr. Rowley would never have done. I did think he would have ask't us all!

Miss G.—I am surprised at what you say, because you have married twice yourself.

Martha J.—To be sure ; and that makes me hate it all the worser.

DAVID EVANS.

Miss G. and David Evans, an old Widower at Llansevern.

Miss G.—I hear that you lost your wife ten years ago. You must have led a sad, lonely life since her death.

David E.—Quite the other way, ma'am. I'd never no peace at all till she went. I prayed to the Lord night and day for thirty years that He would please to part us; but I left it to Him which way it should be. I was quite ready to go myself; but He took her at last, and right thankful I was indeed.

Miss G.—I suppose you were always quarrelling?

David E.—I had a hot temper enough before I was married; but when I see what

an awful woman she was, I says to myself,
' Now, two fires cannot burn together'; and
I grew as quiet as could be, and never con-
trairied her no ways. But she was a most
awful woman; indeed, she did throw a
coffee-pot just off the fire at my head
one day.

Miss G.—I hope she repented before she
died.

David E.—Indeed, I don't know. I did
often say to her when she lay a dying, ' My
dear, I hope the Lord will forgive your sins ;
but I do not know as He will, for you have
been a most awful woman indeed, my dear.'

MARY MORRIS.

Miss G. and Mary Morris, at Llansevern.

Mary Morris.—Well, ma'am, as you say temper is everything, when I was a girl I put a curb on mine, through a thing as took place in a farm-house hard by where I was reared. There was a young woman as lived servant there, by name Mary Jones, and her and a yong man as lived servant along with her was used to get up at four o'clock to brew, and Mary was a bad 'un to get up in a morning, so the yong man, David Williams, was used to throw pebbles up till her window to waken her, and then he used to jeer her a bit about being late, and her didna like it, 'cause her owed him a bit of a grudge (her and him was lovers onst I reckon), so one evening afore brewing day her says to t'other servant girl, as they was going to bed, 'Here, Jane, tak hold o' the end of this stay-lace, and pull me together as hard as ever you can.' So Jane pulled and pulled, and Mary kept saying, 'Harder, Jane, harder,' till Jane was fairly frighted lest her should bosson then and there. 'Now then,' says Mary, 'if I lay me down this a way, I shall be sure to waken every time I stir; I warrant there'll be no occagin for David to be throwing of his nasty pebbles in the morning.' And sure enough there wasn't, for in the morning her was dead just as her lay down, and the blood all con-jellied in her face. There was what come of a proud-sperrited temper!

I often told my step-daughter about it afore her went to service; but her's got married now, silly girl, 'cause her thought work was too hard ; as I said, 'Sarah,' says I, 'where can you show me the service as is as hard as marriage has been to me? Haven't you seen me often enough up at four in the morning and never laying my fingers by till ten o'clock at night?' Why, my husband's such a poor silly piece, that if I didna work my fingers to the bone, the childer 'ud be well-nigh clemmed to death ; however, you know, ma'am, we can't clap our burdens on other folks' backs, specially when we be old and them yong ; so Sarah would be married, say what I would ; but I'll not be deceiving of you, ma'am, for I was married onst afore, as well as my husband, so we was one as foolish as the other.

Miss G.—I don't see that you were so foolish, for John seems a steady, sober man, and pretty good-tempered.

Mary M.—Well, he's not much attached

to the drink, but as for his temper, the less said about it the better ; however, when he's a bit rash, I know when to let my temper drop, and I will say for John Morris he's a very good man for attending his church and bringing home the tex to his family, whether it's long or short. Now there's a deal of difference 'twixt his head and mine, for let me try all as ever I can, the tex is always out of my head afore I'm well down the church steps ; however, I'm scholar enough to read pretty tidy in them tracks as Mr. Palmer brings, and indeed I'do think I can find by what they say in them, here a bit and there a bit, as I'm not altogether quite as perfect as I should be yet ; yes, indeed I do think them tracks finds out the truth.

MRS. JONES.

Miss G. and Mrs. Jones at Llansevern.

Miss G.—Are you a widow?

Mrs. Jones.—I was a widow fifteen years, but I'm not now, more's the silliness. Sit you down, please ma'am, and I'll tell you the foundations of it.

There was an old feller by name John Jones, as lived at Carnarvon, and he was used to come onst a year cross the country to pay his club at Llanfair, and he'd a sister as lived there, so she said to him last summer, 'John,' says she, 'it taks a deal o' shoe-leather and time too for you to travel such a way

7

every summer; I'd make myself a home in these parts if I was you; I know of a nice little badger woman at Llansevern who would make a mighty scrat of a wife for you, and bring you a bit o' money too, for she's had no husband to spend her gettings these fifteen years.' Well, ma'am, the old feller came straight off in a minute, and came and axed me to lodge him a few days. I used to make a pretty good thing of lodgers. So after he'd stopped a few days, he says to me, 'Mrs. Evans, I've been thinking that it 'ud be a mighty good thing if you and me was to put our bit o' money together.' 'What have you got, John Jones?' says I (I always called him that a way). 'Eighty pounds in the bank,' says he, 'and a few pounds in hand besides. What have you got, Mrs. Evans?' 'Fifty,' says I. 'That's not so much,' says the old feller. 'No,' says I; 'but I'm a deal youngerer nor you, John Jones,' says I, 'and may be I shall want your money afore you want mine.' 'May be so,' says he, 'you be a fresh-looking woman of your age.' 'Yes,' says I, 'but when I was young I'd a colour like the rising sun.'

Well, so we agreed upon it ; but I wouldn't be married till we'd been to a lawyer and made a bit of settling. Well, I allowed the old feller two or three days' play after we was married, and then I said, ' John Jones,' says I, 'I'm thinking you'd better not let the grass grow under your feet any longer.' So he went out to see after work ; but he came home and pretended he could not find none, and then another day he'd cotched a cold, and another day and another some nonsense or other, and if you'll believe me, ma'am, in five weeks he only brought me sixpence wrapped up in paper, just as if it was a sovering. 'This is the pounds you had in hand, I reckon, John

Jones,' says I. So after we'd begun to fall out,
I could hear of his canting to the neighbours
and saying the little badger woman well-nigh
starved him ; and then, worst of all, he puts
me in the newspaper for debt, a good-for-
nothing old feller as he was, for all he prayed
and read the Bible terrible. He was all for
them Independents. Mr. Morgan, the preacher,
came to see me after John Jones and me was
parted, and he says to me, 'Never mind, Mrs.
Jones, there's a new law come up as'll give
you leave to marry somebody else if you
wait two years.' ' That law never come out of
the Bible, I know,' says I. ' No matter where
it come from,' says he. There's a fine religion
for you ! I suppose, ma'am, you've heard
about Mrs. Bowen, her whose husband came
back from 'Stralia, after her'd been married
four years to David Evans? Well, Mr.
Morgan did say to her, 'Why need you vex

yourself, Mrs. Bowen; you've got two on 'em, why can't you tak your chice?'

I've been a big fool enough, but I know my Bible better than to say I'm not John Jones's lawful wife, the miserly old feller.

———————

SALLY THOMAS.

Miss G. and Sally Thomas at Llansevern.

Sally Thomas.—I've been very bad these three weeks, ma'am. I was first attackted in my throat, and then my heart got out of the socket; Mr. Johnson did order me to have a blister and six leeches. I put on the blister, but not the leeches, for I judged it was better to leave something for the Lord to do.

Miss G.—Did any of your daughters come to nurse you?

Sally T.—Daughters! they be all married, except them in the churchyard; they be the best off, I reckon.

Miss G.—If your daughters have forsaken

you because they are married, I'm afraid you
could not have brought them up very well.

Sally T.—O yes, but I broke dozens of rods
over them, and they could never see me do
anything as was wrong. I'm not one of them as
says right and hacts contrairy; some of 'em
as does got a fine rebuke in Mr. Hughes's
sermon on Sunday.

Miss G.—What did he say?

Sally T.—Well, I'm no scholar, but I could
tell it was meant for somebody as had done
what he hadn't ought to do; them as has
learned, could tell you well enough what he
meant, but I can't 'splain it.

Miss G.—I think perhaps the reason is, you
are not quite mistress of the English language.

Sally T.—Sure enough then I'm mistress
of none, for I never spoke nothing else. Me
a Welsh woman! No, indeed, thank God!
But I'll tell you how it is as I can't 'splain

things : I know it all in my head, but I've not got the principle of speaking.

Miss G.—I hope your husband behaves better to you than he used to do.

Sally T.—Well, well, he's but a poor miserable creatur ; I'm just like a mouse held in a cat's claw ; and then when he's drunk, I can't sarve him as I used to do, and douk him in a bucket o' water, 'cause now he's in years it 'ud give him the rheumatis, and then there'd be nothing to make the pot boil; there's little enough now, for if the old man gets six or seven shillings he never gives me more than two or three, and 'spects bacon to his taters, and sugar to his tea ; however, there's a better paymaster above, as'll reward me better nor old John, for all my heating and cooling and wetting and drying, summer and winter. I says to him many a time, ' A well o' water's never missed till it's gone dry; and when I'm gone you'll be giving me a character, for all you lay all the blame on the ould woman now.'

Miss G.—If I were you, I should try to mend him a little before you die.

Sally T.—Mend him, indeed! No, no, the evil has got such fast hold of his inside that it will never let him loose i' this world, I'm sartain sure.

———————

A DONKEY BOY.

Miss G., in a donkey-chair at Rhyl, and Tom Powell, aged fifteen, running by the side of the donkey.

Miss G.—This seems a nice quiet donkey.

Tom.—Yes! in the chair; but if you was to go into his stable at feeding time you would soon be a dead woman; and he'll finish me some day, I expect. He often catches me with his teeth on each side of my ribs, and begins shaking the breath out of my body. So then I have to thump as hard as I can with my two fisses on his back-bone; and I haven't a chance, because my arms is weak through having been broken to bits and pierced again two or three times. A donkey as I knew in Manchester killed three men, and bit off the arm of another clean away at the shoulder. So then his master shot him; for he said that he might get into trouble through him. I was reared in Manchester.

Miss G.—Are you a good scholar?

Tom.—Well, I'm not so particular at reading; but I'd cast with anybody. I'll engage you'll never meet one as could beat me. Pounds or pence—it's all one to me. I'd cast all the figures in the world and never be a penny the wrong. There's for ye!

I won't take you down that street, for it is the blackguardingist place as I ever heard tell of. If you put your foot over the door-sill to go out, you can't draw the other after it afore somebody shies broken glass or crockery at you. We'll go on the Parade.

Now look sharp, ma'am; there's a ginger-coloured 'oss with the carriage painted to match him. And it's a queer-built thing, too, with wings down to the ground. Well,

I do declare! they've gone and put a pair
of 'osses—and thundering bigs 'uns too—in
that light carriage as you might draw yourself. And then, look ye now! that great
lumbering thing as is all timber and no
wheels has got but one poor skin-and-bone
'oss. How contrairy they does things in Rhyl!

That lady there is a queer one. The
first day I took her on the sands, her kept
saying, 'I can see nothing.' 'Well,' says I,
'to be sure, ma'am, sand is sand; but there
can't be splendider fields of it nowhere.'
So then her told me to take her down to
the sea at low water. So I says, 'I will, if
you like; but you won't come back in the
same fashion you go, for the donkey will
soon be plundering in a bog, and the chair
set quite fast; and then you must get out
and lay yourself flat on your face, and hold
fast with both hands to one end of a hand-

kerchief, and, then I should tie the other end round my leg, and lay me down on my face just before you, and flounder and paddle with my arms and legs till I'd drawed you over the bog. That's the way we always serves ladies as gets bogged. Your legs goes down like pins into a pincushion ; but when you're spread out it takes a long time to suck you in.' So then her said no more about the sea ; but her kept on murmuring as her could see nothing, and when I pointed to a gull or a flag-staff for her to look at, her thought I was a mocking of her. She was quite curous one day in the town. Her would go out in the chair when it was a showering and a powering as hard as it could, and every time the wind blew the rain in her face her fell into a pet with me, and said I was taking her in the face of the rain a-purpose, and she made me turn first down one street and then another, till we had gone miles and miles ; and I'm sure when I got home I squeezed three quarts of water out of my jacket—pilot-cloth holds it, you know.

Look, ma'am ! how plain we can see Anglesey. I'm a thinking whether they can see the coast here. I should say they could. What do you think, ma'am ?

It was at that there corner that the *Royal Charter* was wrecked. A woman in Rhyl had two sons aboard, and one of them was saved ; but he had been so long in the water that his skin came off all in one cake. The doctor perceived it quite loose, so he just nicked it down the back-bone and turned the skin off right and left just as you would an orange. And then he cured the skin, and his mother lapped it up in a cupboard. It looks for all the world like bathing-caps. The other son as was drownded wasn't washed up for a month. He had a belt round him with his name at full length cut on it, and a bag with seventy sovereigns inside it; but his head and arms and legs were all washed away. So his mother said, 'Seventy sovereigns—no! nor twice seventy—should not make her own to such a poor battered thing as that for her son.' So she made them carry off the body and the belt and money and all. She was working hard enough for a living; so there was stupid foolishness for you! I wonder what sort of a skiliton it must be as I wouldn't own for the sake of seventy pounds!

Do you think it's true, ma'am, as there's a new church on a rock out yonder, as they can only walk to at low water? Mus'n't them as built it have been downright soft 'uns, if they expected folks to pay money for boats to take 'em to church instead of a-pleasuring! If I was inside there at high-water, and there was to come a storm, I should fall on my knees pretty sharp; and I'm thinking may be it was to frighten folks into saying their prayers harder as 'ticed them to build the church.

Them lifeboats is curous things, ma'am. The men as mans the boat is stuffed into holes in the deck, the very same as putting corks into bottles, so that they can't come out when they are topsy-turvy; and they say when a storm comes on, and they are short of hands, they can force any gentle-man, or even a Duke or Prince, to come. My sake! how queer a grand one must feel when his legs go down into the hole, and he can see no more of them!

THE END.